P9-AOE-054

Dear Parents and Educators,

Welcome to Penguin Young Readers! As parents and educators, you know that each child develops at his or her own pace—in terms of speech, critical thinking, and, of course, reading. Penguin Young Readers recognizes this fact. As a result, each Penguin Young Readers book is assigned a traditional easy-to-read level (1–4) as well as a Guided Reading Level (A–P). Both of these systems will help you choose the right book for your child. Please refer to the back of each book for specific leveling information. Penguin Young Readers features esteemed authors and illustrators, stories about favorite characters, fascinating nonfiction, and more!

Pearl and Wagner: Four Eyes

LEVEL 3

GUIDED READING LEVEL K

This book is perfect for a **Transitional Reader** who:

- can read multisyllable and compound words;
- can read words with prefixes and suffixes;
- is able to identify story elements (beginning, middle, end, plot, setting, characters, problem, solution); and
- can understand different points of view.

Here are some **activities** you can do during and after reading this book:

- Character Traits: Pearl is Wagner's best friend. In this story, Pearl shows us how to be a good friend. Write down some of Pearl's traits that make her such a good friend.
- Problem/Solution: In this story, Wagner is unable to read the nurse's writing on the board. This is the problem. The solution to this problem is Wagner getting glasses. Discuss another problem in this story, and the solution to Wagner's problem.

Remember, sharing the love of reading with a child is the best gift you can give!

—Bonnie Bader, EdM
Penguin Young Readers program

*Penguin Young Readers are leveled by independent reviewers applying the standards developed by Irene Fountas and Gay Su Pinnell in *Matching Books to Readers: Using Leveled Books in Guided Reading*, Heinemann, 1999.

For the Wilson girls: Sadie Louise, Miller Kate, and Josephine—KM

To Mrs. Huntington, who took an interest in my drawing once I got glasses—RWA

Penguin Young Readers
Published by the Penguin Group
Penguin Group (USA) Inc., 375 Hudson Street, New York, New York 10014, USA
Penguin Group (Canada), 90 Eglinton Avenue East, Suite 700, Toronto, Ontario M4P 2Y3, Canada
(a division of Pearson Penguin Canada Inc.)
Penguin Books Ltd, 80 Strand, London WC2R 0RL, England
Penguin Ireland, 25 St Stephen's Green, Dublin 2, Ireland (a division of Penguin Books Ltd)
Penguin Group (Australia), 707 Collins Street, Melbourne, Victoria 3008, Australia
(a division of Pearson Australia Group Pty Ltd)
Penguin Books India Pvt Ltd, 11 Community Centre, Panchsheel Park, New Delhi—110 017, India
Penguin Group (NZ), 67 Apollo Drive, Rosedale, Auckland 0632, New Zealand
(a division of Pearson New Zealand Ltd)
Penguin Books (South Africa), Rosebank Office Park, 181 Jan Smuts Avenue,
Parktown North 2193, South Africa
Penguin China, B7 Jiaming Center, 27 East Third Ring Road North,
Chaoyang District, Beijing 100020, China

Penguin Books Ltd, Registered Offices: 80 Strand, London WC2R 0RL, England

The original art was created using pen and ink, watercolor, and a few colored pencils on Strathmore Bristol.

 First published in 2009 by Dial Books for Young Readers, an imprint of Penguin Group (USA) Inc. Published in 2013 by Penguin Young Readers, an imprint of Penguin Group (USA) Inc., 345 Hudson Street, New York, New York 10014. Manufactured in China.

The Library of Congress has cataloged the Dial edition under the following Control Number:
2009050788

ISBN 978-0-448-47781-7 10 9 8 7 6 5 4 3 2 1

Pearl and Wagner
Four Eyes

by Kate McMullan
pictures by R. W. Alley

Penguin Young Readers
An Imprint of Penguin Group (USA) Inc.

Contents

Hey Pearl!
What, Wagner?
Why did the teacher wear sunglasses?
I give up - why?

Because her pupils were so bright!

VOCAB QUIZ ON TUESDAY
EYE TEST
Brain
eye ball
Iris
Pupil

Chapter 1
Raw Bird Pizza

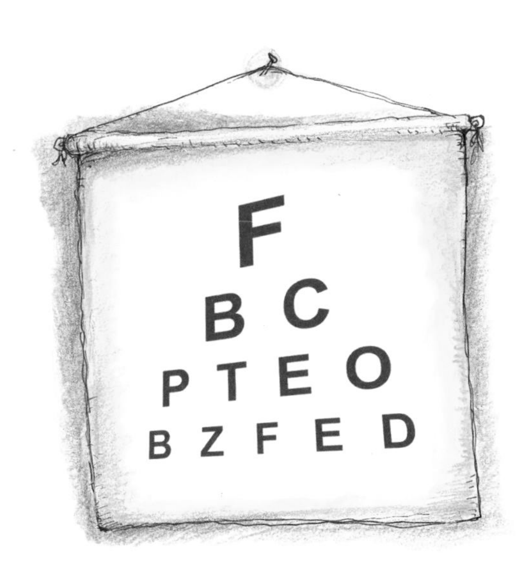

On Monday morning, Nurse Nice came into Ms. Star's classroom.

She wrote on the board:

Eye Test Today.

Wagner squinted and read, "Eye . . . Toast . . . Toady."

"Uh-oh," said Pearl.

Nurse Nice put tape on the floor.

She hung a chart on the wall.

“Line up for your eye test!” she said.

Pearl was first in line.

Wagner was right behind her.

Last in line was Ms. Star.

"Cover your right eye and read from the top," said Nurse Nice.

Pearl covered her eye.

"G, W, V, G, S, B, E," she read.

"Left eye," said Nurse Nice.

"Keep going."

"N, O, I, H, W," read Pearl.

"Your eyes are fine," said Nurse Nice.

"J, H, E, R, L, C," Pearl read quickly.

"N, O, S, Z, L, E, P, H, U, L, Y, T, H."

"Next!" said Nurse Nice.

Nurse Nice flipped the chart over.
"Cover your right eye and read
from the top," she said.
Wagner covered his eye.
"E," he read. "B? No, wait. P!"
"Left eye," said Nurse Nice.

"E!" Wagner read.

He blinked.

"E . . ." he read again.

He shut his eyes

and shouted, "E, I, E, I, O!"

After the eye test,

Nurse Nice gave Wagner a note

to take home.

“You need to see an eye doctor,”

she said.

“Who, me?” said Wagner.

At recess, Lulu said,

“Do you have to get glasses, Wag?”

“No way,” said Wagner.

Pearl pointed across the street.

"Read the red sign," she said.

Wagner squinted.

"Raw Bird Pizza," he read.

"Glasses time!" said Pearl.

Chapter 2
Wagner's New Look

Pearl and Wagner walked
home from school together.
"I wish *I* needed glasses," said Pearl.
"Glasses can give you a whole
new look."

They passed Ron & Bert's Pizza.
Next to it was Gayle's Glasses Shop.
Pearl pointed to a pair of glasses
in the window.
"If I wore these glasses,
I'd look like a rock star!" she said.
"You think so?" asked Wagner.

Pearl pointed to another pair.

"In these, I'd look like a scientist,"

said Pearl.

"Right," said Wagner.

"A mad scientist."

"These would make me look like an actor," said Pearl.

"Pearl—starring in *Swamp Monster*!" said Wagner.

"Cut it out!" said Pearl.

"Sorry," said Wagner.

"But you don't even need glasses."

"Oh, right," Pearl said.

Pearl studied the glasses again.

"Don't worry, Wag," she said.

"I will find a great new look for you."

"I like my old look," said Wagner.

"I am never getting glasses.

Never, never, never!"

The next Monday morning,
Wagner waited for Pearl on the corner.
"What's wrong?" said Pearl
when she saw him.
"I got glasses," said Wagner.

"Put them on!" Pearl said.

"No," said Wagner.

"I hate my glasses.

They pinch my nose.

They poke the backs of my ears.

They make me look like a guppy."

"Let *me* put them on!" said Pearl.

"You asked for it," said Wagner.
He took the glasses out of his
backpack and gave them to Pearl.

"Everything is fuzzy," said Pearl.

She tried to walk.

"I feel dizzy! And sick!"

She turned to Wagner.

"But how do I look?" she asked.

Wagner squinted at Pearl.

"Blurry," he said.

Pearl gave Wagner his glasses back.

"Put them on, Wag," she said.

"I will tell you how you look."

Wagner put on his glasses.

Pearl gasped.

“You look so cool,” she said.

“I do?” said Wagner.

“You do,” said Pearl. “Come on! Let’s show Lulu and Bud and Henry.”

She grabbed his arm and they ran to school.

Chapter 3
Four-Eyes Pizza

When they reached the playground,
Pearl called, “Wagner got glasses!”
Everybody ran over to see.

"You look great," said Lulu.

"You look smart," said Bud.

"You look like

Wagner with glasses,"

said Henry.

"Thanks," said Wagner.

Just then two big boys
came over to Wagner.
One boy said, "Hi, Four Eyes!"
The other boy laughed
as they walked off.

"Phooey!" said Wagner.
"Now I am Four Eyes!"

He whipped off his glasses
and threw them into his
backpack.

“I have on a hat,” said Henry.

“I guess that makes me Two Heads.”

“I’m wearing boots,” said Bud.

“That makes me Four Feet.”

Wagner smiled.

“I have on a scarf,” said Lulu.

“I’m Two Necks!”

Pearl waggled her gloves and said,

“Twenty Fingers!”

Wagner put his glasses back on.

“The name’s Four Eyes,” he said.

The bell rang and they all
ran into the classroom.
Ms. Star was writing on the board.
"'Pizza Party Today'!" read Wagner.
"Hooray!" said Bud.

"Why are we having a party?"
asked Pearl.
"To celebrate seeing," said Ms. Star.
She turned around.

Everybody gasped.
"Wow!" said Pearl.
"You look like Ms. Rock Star!"